oah Ramsbottom
and the
Cave Elves

Rob Bullock

Strategic Book Publishing
New York, New York

Strategic Book Publishing
An imprint of AEG Publishing Group
845 Third Avenue, 6th Floor – 6016
New York, NY 10022
http://www.strategicbookpublishing.com

ISBN: 978-1-60860-335-0

Printed in the United States of America

Book Design: Suzanne Kelly

More stories from Rob Bullock—www.ninnylizard.com

For Kristen with love

Noah Ramsbottom and
the Cave Elves

"JUST . . . ONE . . . MORE . . . STRETCH!" thought Noah. "Err, grab that rock and I'm there! It's got to be up here! Got to be!"

Noah Ramsbottom was eight and, like his grandad, he was an explorer.

It was a month since Grandad had mysteriously disappeared; he had gone out walking one morning and nobody had seen him since. The papers said it was a mystery and even the mountain rescue teams said they couldn't imagine where he'd gone.

Grandad used to tell everyone about his adventures—stories about elves and pixies, savage monsters and fierce machines. He told stories of the strange worlds and places he'd visited. Everyone thought he was just a silly old man—a bit barking, they said—but Noah didn't think so. Noah believed his grandad. Grandad would never lie to him.

"But Mum," cried Noah just before they had left the farmhouse that morning, "Grandad couldn't just disappear. He's an explorer, and the first rule of exploring is finding your way home!"

"Maybe he got confused, sweetheart," replied his tearful mum. "He's an old man. Maybe he slipped and fell somewhere, maybe into a stream, maybe into a deep cave or pothole. You do read about these things."

"Mum!" yelled Noah. "Grandad was a good explorer. Maybe he's not lost after all. Maybe he can't get home."

"What do you mean?"

"Maybe someone has taken him prisoner?"

"What? Who would do such a thing? You've been listening to his daft stories for too long, my lad! What an imagination! Your grandad's missing and you'll have to be brave and understand he might never come home, my love."

Since Grandad had disappeared, the winter weather had been bad. Even the rescue people could hardly manage to get out to look for him. But today the weather was dry—cold, but dry. Noah could take the chance of trying to find Grandad.

"Don't go too far!" yelled Mum.

"Okay!" Noah called over his shoulder.

As Noah heaved himself over the last rocky ledge with all his strength, he saw it for the first time.

"This must be Victoria Cave!" he gasped.

"Victoria Cave! Victoria Cave! No such place! Cave of Victoria more like!" squeaked a small voice.

"What! Who said that?"

"Who said *that?*" it squeaked again.

"I did!"

"Who is 'I'? Who be there? Tell me at once who this 'I' be! *Stop!* Don't look around or else!"

"Ouch! That hurts. What's that?"

"That be my flubblestick 'I'… *Stop!* Don't look around! Now tell me who is this 'I' who be appeared, or 'I' will feel more than just the tip of my flubblestick!"

"Er, I'm Noah Ramsbottom. Please don't use that flub … er?"

"Flubblestick."

"Yeah, flubblestick."

"What be 'I', er, Noah Ramsbottom wanting with the Cave of Victoria?"

3

"I'm looking for my grandad. He's lost, you see, and I've come to find him and rescue him!"

"Who be this human person, 'I' … er?"

"Noah."

"Yes, 'I', er, me means Noah Ramsbum? He-he-he, Ramsbum be a very funny name Mr. 'I', tee hee."

"No it's not!" said Noah firmly. "It's not funny at all, and it's Ramsbottom, and it's a proper name."

"Er, sorry, Mr. 'I', er, Noah. You can turn around if you like."

"Wow! What! A *real* pixie!" Noah said, looking down on a very small, very strange man in a security guard uniform that was too big for his bony little body. There was a cap perched on pointy, sticky-out ears, and he had a large, sharp nose.

"Not pixie," said the small man, spitting on the ground in disgust. "A real *elf!*"

"Oh, sorry, a real elf! What's your name Mr. Elf?"

"Me name's Littleplod, Xzgrxxrg Littleplod, but Xzgrxxrg is hard for human people to say, so you can call me Mr. Littleplod."

"Nice to meet you, Mr. Littleplod," said Noah, stretching down to shake hands.

"Wow! It's bigger than I thought it would be," said Noah, walking slowly forward into the entrance of the big cave.

"WOAWOAWOAWOA!" wailed a deafening siren.

"What's that noise?" said Noah, covering his ears.

"Quickly, I Noah, come with me!" said Littleplod, yanking on Noah's hand.

"What is it, what's the noise for?"

"It be a warning, I Noah!"

"Noah, just Noah, not *I Noah!* Warning about what?"

"Sorry, I, er, Just Noah. It be a sky raid! Quick, behind here!"

Littleplod scurried to a small hole in the cave wall, dragging Noah behind him.

Littleplod yelled over his shoulder, "Watch out for—"

"Ouch! For rocks? I think I've just hit my leg on one. Ow, that really hurt!" Noah said, rubbing his shin.

"Behind here, Noah!" Littleplod said from behind a boulder.

Ack, Ack, Ack, Ack! Guns were firing mushroom bullets into the sky. *Ack, Ack, Ack!*

Swoosh! Massive birds were dive-bombing the cave—except that they weren't birds at all: they were flying machines.

"What are they? Some kind of robot birds?"

"They be Robocrows!"

"But why are they attacking Victoria Cave?"

"Cave of Victoria be the home of the Cave Elves and Cave Elves be at war with them."

"With Robocrows?"

"No, stupid Just Noah, not with Robocrows; they be just machines!"

"Then who then? Who sent the Robocrows?"

"Swamptrolls!"

"Swamptrolls? What are Swamptrolls?"

"Why do human peoples always repeat what is said to them?"

"I thought that this was just a cave on the side of this crag! Sorry!"

"Thinking be getting your grandad captured, that's what thinking be doing!"

"So you do know Grandad?"

BANNNGGG! A flying bomb exploded on the cave floor just in front of Noah and Littleplod, covering everything in stuff that looked a lot like old egg yolk.

"Egg bombs, too? Poo! They stink!" said Noah, pinching his nose.

"Egg bombs be stinking out the whole place!" agreed Littleplod.

"Grandad? Where is Grandad?"

"Grandad Fred be captured by the enemy of both Cave Elves and Swamptrolls, the Furglegurgles."

"Furglegurgles? You've got to be kidding me, you're making it all up! You're just a weird little tramp who lives up here in the crags in your funny stolen uniform that's way too big for you."

"It be fitting perfect, Noah Ramsbottom, and I be a Cave Elf. In fact I be the Cave Guard, Xzgrxxg Littleplod! I'll have you know, Furglegurgles be real, Swamptrolls be real and stinking egg bombs be real, too!"

The stink was terrible, a cross between rotten eggs and cow poo!

"Poo! Well, the egg bombs smell real enough, and I did see the Robocrows with my own eyes. Maybe you're not a tramp after all."

"There be nothing wrong with tramps."

"I never said there was!"

"Tramps be good friends of Cave Elves. They be Cave Elf spies, spying on human peoples!"

"Tramps are spies?"

"Always repeating, be human people!"

WOAWOAWOAWOA! wailed a deafening siren once more as the bombing seemed to have stopped.

"All clear, I Noah Ramsbottom, the repeating human person."

"I'm just repeating because all of this— this place, you, the Robocrows, Grandad a prisoner—it's just too much to think about!"

Littleplod put a comforting arm around Noah's waist (he couldn't reach his shoulders).

"Be not worrying, Noah. We be finding Grandad Fred, and we be rescuing him!"

"Rescuing Grandad? Really? When? Can we go now?"

"Now be a good time for rescuing, Littleplod be thinking. Too smelly out here; let the Cleaning Elves clean up the mess. If Littleplod be here, he be getting a scrubbing brush and a bucket! Littleplod not be liking cleaning! Be following, I Noah!"

"Noah, *just Noah!*"

"Righteo Noah Just Noah!"

Littleplod led Noah deep into the cavern.

"What is this place?" asked Noah as they walked carefully into the cavern. "It's huge!

"Cave of Victoria, Noah Ramsbottom, be a magic cave, and it be very magicky indeed," said Littleplod solemnly.

"What's magic about it?"

As Noah cautiously picked his way over the stinking egg that covered the ground, from down below he heard his worried mum shouting for him.

"Noah! Noah! Are you alright, Noah?"

Noah turned and scurried back to the ledge he'd scrambled over just moments before. He knelt down on the grass and peered over. It was a long way down; he must have climbed a long way. He could see his mum far down below in the valley bottom.

"Hi Mum, I'm just up here exploring. Is it okay if I play up here for a while?" he shouted through cupped hands.

"Have you got your phone?"

Noah felt in his pocket.

"Yeah!"

"Well, alright, but you just be careful, and you be home by three, do you hear me, Noah Ramsbottom? No later than three!"

"Yeah!" called Noah, getting back to his feet and rushing back into the depths of the cave.

"Oi! Noah Ramsbottom, you be clumsy— nearly knocked Littleplod over cliff edge!" grumbled the little man.

"Sorry, I didn't see you down there. I didn't do it on purpose."

"Apologings be accepted, but more careful be in future!"

"Wow, it's amazing in here," Noah said, gazing all around.

"It be all real gold and jewels, I Noah."

As Noah looked up, a shimmering shower of golden petals floated to the ground and, instead of a dark cave, there was a brightly lit chamber. Dozens of little elves were to-ing and fro-ing about their daily business. Most were dressed like workmen and women. Others had smart suits on and were carrying clipboards. These elves were bossing the others about. The Work Elves had brightly coloured overalls on, some had hard hats on, others tiny caps with badges with the letters EMC on the front.

Some of the Work Elves were carrying tool-boxes and others were sitting on strange clockwork mechanical digging contraptions.

"Beep, Beep! Beep, Beep! Be making way for Elf Cleaning Squad 14!" bellowed a voice.

Noah and Littleplod jumped to the side as an orange-coloured buggy with a gigantic, slow-turning key on the front rushed past. The buggy was overflowing with elves in yellow overalls, wellies and rubber gloves.

"They be Cleanings Elves!"

"So I see," nodded Noah.

When Noah looked further into the cave, he could see other elves busy doing all kinds of things. In one small corner, some of the Work Elves sat about eating their lunch. They were eating tiny sandwiches and drinking from minute cups. An elf in a black suit and a bowler hat was yelling at them to get back to work.

"Do human people have bossy people telling them what to do?" asked Littleplod.

"Oh yes," replied Noah. "We call them bosses!"

"Bosses?"

"Yeah. Wh, what are all these elves doing?"

"Ttt! They be opening up, of course!"

"Opening up what?"

"New doorways. What else be there?"

"Why?" asked Noah.

"Why what, I?"

"Why are they opening up new doorways?"

"Because the Elf Mining Company told them to be, of course!"

Littleplod proudly thrust out the EMC badge that was on his jacket.

"And why did the Elf Mining Company tell them to do it?"

"Doesn't Just I Noah Ramsbottom be knowing anything?" asked Littleplod, staring up at Noah, who towered above him.

"I know lots of things," Noah replied, a little hurt.

"As I be saying before, this be a magic cave, Just I Noah Ramsbottom, and each new opening be having a special doorway."

"Special doorways? Will we find Grandad through one of them?"

"We be surely trying to find Grandad Fred."

"Mr. Littleplod. Where do they go to, these special doorways?"

"I be showing you, if you like."

"Yes, please!" Noah said, nodding vigorously.

"We needs to be careful though. Miss Bagshot be sacking Littleplod if she finds out, you being an official human person and not an official elf person. But I is from a family of explorers too,

Just I Noah, and Grandad Fred is a good friend of mine. Come on, follow me. We need to hurry!"

The elf started walking really fast into the cave. Noah had to run to keep up with him even though he was three times the size of the little man. When they had just entered a tiny way into the huge cavern, the little man turned sharply to his left. Noah was surprised to see a small, ancient-looking heavy wooden door guarding an entrance that had been cut into the damp cave walls. The door was just a bit bigger than Noah, so he wouldn't have to duck. It had a large, golden *Number 1* on it and a heavy, iron door handle—a bit like a latch on a garden gate. To the right of it was another door and beside that another, and then another. In fact, there were dozens and dozens of doors stretching back deep into the cavern.

Littleplod lifted the latch and pushed the door open. Its rusty old hinges squeaked. Noah noticed that the elf had a tiny notepad and a pencil sticking out of the top pocket of his smart little guard's uniform. The guard took out

the pencil, licked the tip, and wrote, speaking at the same time:

"Be telling Maintenance, oiling hinges door Number 1!"

He looked up at Noah, smiled and said, "You be having to be keeping on top of Maintenance you know, or nothing be getting done!"

Noah politely laughed a little laugh and curiously followed the elf as he walked through the small doorway. As Noah walked into the room he let out a little "Wow!" He stared, his eyes wide open. In front of him was a truly magical world.

"Wow!" he said again. "This is a-m-a-zing!"

"It be magicmazing!" said Littleplod, in that way he had of making up words.

Noah and Littleplod stood in the open doorway looking across a huge, prehistoric valley. They could see for miles and miles. There were forests full of strange-looking trees, rivers, and lakes. In the distance were sharp, pointed mountains with snow on top. Gone were the familiar grassy hills and limestone crags that he had been climbing up just a few minutes ago. Here was a world of swamps and trees and, just below them, a beautiful, emerald-green lake.

Suddenly out of the lake rose a tiny, moving head. Gradually more and more of a long, sleek neck followed. Slowly, a huge body lumbered out. A tail longer than two buses swooshed to the rear. The creature plodded along with thunderous steps, splashing water everywhere, to the shore and snacked greedily on some tasty tree tops.

"A . . . a dino . . . dino . . . dinosaur!" gasped Noah in a small, weak voice. His knees were shaking and he could hardly stand up.

"Be Diplodocus!" said Littleplod knowledge-ably, his chest puffed out proudly.

"Yeah!" agreed Noah.

"Littleplod be knowing his monsters!"

High above him Noah could see Pteranodons gliding gracefully around in the blue sky, their long, bony wings almost as wide as a jet plane. They were circling high in the sky, screeching loudly, peering down at the strange world below.

On the ground in front of him, Noah saw something familiar lying on a little ledge just in

front of his feet. He knelt down and picked up the old chewed pipe.

"Grandad's pipe!" he said. "Grandad must be here!"

"We must ask the Naggledongs where Grandad Fred be."

"Naggledongs? Are you serious?"

"Littleplod never jokes about his friends!"

"Friends? What are these Naggledongs then?"

"They be the fairies that live in this world. They be the Cave Elves' cousins!"

"So where are they?"

"I be blowing on my special whistle and they be surely appearing!"

"Go on then, let's see it, blow your whistle and make these Naggledongs appear."

Littleplod proudly pulled a shiny silver whistle out of his pocket, put it to his lips and blew into it with all his might.

Psssssssss, came out the feeble noise.

"Not very good at whistling, are you?"

Psssssssss, Littleplod tried again.

There was no sign of any Naggledong fairies. But Littleplod had gotten the attention of the munching Diplodocus, who was staring right at them curiously.

"Well, *he* heard you alright!" said Noah.

Thud, thud, thud. Now the ground around them was shaking. The shaking was getting stronger and stronger, almost knocking Noah off his feet. The creature that was making the ground shake was getting closer and closer. Littleplod started tugging at his sleeve.

"Oh yes, I Noah, I think something else might have heard the whistle too!"

"Something that's coming right our way!" agreed Noah.

"Noah Ramsbottom, this be bad, be very bad. Must be going, going out through door Number 1!"

"We're not going back without Grandad! We've got to find him!"

"But it be dangerous here. We be lunch for something horrible!"

Noah was shaking with fear, but he knew he had to find Grandad. Suddenly something was tugging at his clothes. When Noah looked down, a handful of fairies had gathered around him and Littleplod. They were tiny; even Littleplod towered over them.

"Come quickly, Dragon comes. Dragon bad."

"We should be going with them I Noah!"

"Sounds like a good idea to me, but where to?"

"Always questions, human person. Just be getting in one of the baskets."

Littleplod was pointing to a small straw basket that looked a lot like the one Noah's mum used for the shopping. The basket had handles that were attached to thin ropes.

"That! I can't get into that—it's too small, and besides, it'll break because I'm too heavy."

"Well, I be getting in one. Bye bye, Just I Noah Ramsbum, Dragon lunch!"

"Stop! Wait for me!" Noah squeezed himself uncomfortably into the basket and four fairies heaved and pushed them until they started moving.

Just as they started to move, the fairies leapt into the basket and, as they did, a tall tree a few metres away suddenly crashed to the ground.

"ROAR!"

The sound was deafening! It was like thunder! Noah covered his ears with his hands, his head hurt, and his whole body rattled from head to toe. Out of nowhere, a huge, tooth-filled head appeared. A black eye was looking right at him.

"Argh!" screamed Noah.

Argh!" screamed the four fairies from the bottom of the basket.

But the basket was moving quickly and just as the powerful jaws of the creature snapped shut with a huge thud, they zoomed out of its reach and through the forest.

"Weeeeeee!" yelled the fairies.

"Fantastic!" yelled Noah as they whizzed through the dense trees. The basket swung wildly from side to side as it shot around corners. Under fallen logs and over giant mushrooms they flew. Suddenly Noah felt lighter, much lighter.

"Jump!" yelled a familiar voice.

Noah did as he was told and forced himself out of the basket just as it crashed into a massive mound of logs.

Noah rolled and landed on a soft pile of raked leaves.

"Tee hee! I Noah nearly become I Squashed Noah!" laughed Littleplod.

"Thanks for the warning," said Noah, dusting himself off.

They were in a huge opening and were surrounded by a crowd of Naggledong fairies.

"My fairy cousin Weenyplod tells me Grandad Fred is up in the Pteranodon nest!" said Littleplod pointing up a sheer rock face that towered above them.

"How did he get up there?"

"Weenyplod says that when Grandad Fred was captured by the Furglegurgles, they brought him through the forest on the way to their swamp castle. But just as they were climbing onto their boats a giant Pteranodon swooped from the sky and grabbed him. They watched her fly up to that nest with him."

"Wow! But how can we get up to rescue him?"

"Weenyplod here is an inventor, like all my family," Littleplod said proudly. "He has invented a flying machine."

"Really, I hope his flying machine is better than your whistle!"

"Littleplod be not hearing that!"

"Sorry, go on."

"He be telling me his machine can fly you and him up to the nest."

"Great, let's go then!"

"*Not* great, I Noah."

"Why not?"

"Littleplod be saying the machine can fly you up to the nest, but one fairy, one small human person and one Grandad Fred be too heavy to bring down."

"Oh! A problem."

"It be a problem alright."

"Problem!" twittered the crowd of fairies.

"I know!" said Noah

"Know!" copied the crowd.

"Parachute!"

"Parachute!" came the twittering echo.

"But you only be a small human person, I Noah!"

"Small human person," sighed the crowd, all shaking heads at once.

"But Grandad was a soldier."

"Grandad soldier!" came the echo from the crowd.

"Be shutting your fairy gobs!" yelled a furious Littleplod.

"Ohhhhhhh," muttered the shocked crowd, raising their arms, hands dangling.

Weenyplod was tugging at Littleplod's arm. Littleplod bent down and Weenyplod whispered in his ear.

"Weenyplod says if we sew together all the dried lily pads, he thinks it would make a good parachute. And he's got plenty of string!"

"Let's make it, then!" said Noah.

All the fairies helped, pushing and shoving each other to grab pieces of string and leaves, and gradually one lily pad was sewn to another. Long lengths of string were attached and, finally, the parachute was ready.

Noah carefully folded it up.

"Weenyplod be ready, I Noah!" shouted Littleplod.

Littleplod stood beside Weenyplod and a rusty old bumper car which had four old rowing boat oars strapped to a pole that was sticking out of it.

"That's it?" asked Noah, a little afraid.

"That certainly be it, I Noah!" said Littleplod proudly.

"It flies? How does it work?"

"It flies because it be a flying machine, of course. Get in and I be winding up this big key on the front. Hurry up now, before Grandad Fred becomes a bird's dinner."

Weenyplod was already in the bumper car. He was wearing a leather flying cap with large round goggles placed over his eyes. Noah, holding tightly to the parachute, wedged himself behind. Littleplod started winding the key. Faster and faster he wound. Suddenly he jumped free and the machine lurched to life.

The oars turned slowly at first, then quicker and then they became a blur. They took off. Hovering a little at first, then forward, then back, as Weenyplod became familiar with flying.

"Have you done this before?" Noah shouted to Weenyplod.

"No!" squeaked his tiny voice.

"Good luck!" yelled a small voice from the ground.

"Good luck!" echoed dozens of other voices.

"Shut it!" yelled Littleplod. "Only one minute of power!" his voice was becoming fainter.

Noah was worried. But the bumper car *was* flying. Suddenly they rose up out of the trees and then higher and higher. They headed straight for the cliff face and the nest.

As they got closer, Noah could see the faint outline of a man in the nest. Then the man looked up, startled by the noise. He started waving. Noah waved back.

"I knew you'd come," shouted Grandad, grinning from ear to ear.

"I've come to rescue you!" Noah shouted back.

"Be careful."

They closed in on the nest until they were right on top of it.

"Quick," shouted Grandad, "one's hatching and I think I'm its lunch."

"We've got to parachute down!"

"Parachute? I can't!"

"But you were a soldier?"

"I was in the army."

"A soldier?"

"A cook!"

"No?!"

"Watch out, the mother Pteranodon is coming back."

"Jump!" yelled Weenyplod. "I'll distract it!"

"Thanks!" shouted Noah as he leapt out of the flying bumper car smack bang into the nest. Weenyplod banked the bumper car sharply away from the nest and dived quickly into the dark forest below with the Pteranodon following, schreeching angrily.

Grandad hugged Noah.

"It's great to see you, son."

"Great to see you too, Grandad."

"Right, where's this parachute then? I don't fancy hanging around here much longer!"

They unravelled the lily pad parachute and wrapped the strings tightly around themselves, tying them with a tight knot.

"Should we try it out?" asked Noah.

"No time like the present, I suppose."

"Three, two, one!" they yelled together as they leapt into thin air.

The parachute opened perfectly and they soared above the canopy of trees. Behind them they could hear the whirr of the flying bumper car as it dropped back to earth and the screech of the mother Pteranodon as she chased Weenyplod.

"Over here!" yelled a voice from the ground. It was Littleplod and he was beside the open magic door.

Grandad and Noah got the hang of the parachute and floated down to land beside the Cave Elf. Just before they landed, Littleplod grabbed them and they soared all the way through door Number 1 and back into the bustling cave entrance. The door slammed shut. Grandad, Noah, and

Littleplod landed, bump, on their bottoms on the hard floor.

"G-Good landing!" stuttered Noah, puffing hard.

"Thank you, Mr. Littleplod," said Grandad.

"Greetings, Grandad Fred."

After a few minutes, they had all calmed down and caught their breath, and were feeling much perkier.

"Can we go home, Grandad?" asked Noah.

"Noah, I'm sorry, I can't go home, not yet anyway."

"Why not?" Noah asked, disappointed.

"A few days before the Furglegurgles captured me they took my friends Len and Annie—you know them, Len and Annie from Duke Street."

"I didn't know they were missing?"

"That's because I told everyone they were visiting their grandchildren in New Zealand, that's why."

"Oh!"

"So I've got to go and rescue them."

"Where are they?"

"I don't know. I started with door Number 1, and I guess I'll look through door Number 2 next."

"Can I come and help you?"

"You can come back tomorrow, but for now you'd better be going home. Your mum will be worried about where you are."

Noah gave his grandad a big hug and watched as he opened door Number 2. Hot sand blew in as Grandad Fred stepped through and was gone.

When Noah and Littleplod turned around, an indignant little lady elf was staring at them. She had a clipboard in her hand and was tapping it with a tiny pencil.

"Cave Guard, what be this? I be not told of any visitings scheduled for today!"

Littleplod gulped nervously. "Er, I be really sorry, Miss Bagshot. It be just. . ."

"It be just what?" shouted Miss Bagshot, making Noah jump.

"Miss Bagshot. I. . . . I be just showing Noah Ramsbottom—he was looking for Grandad Fred you know, behind the doorways!"

Noah could see that Littleplod was really scared. He knew he could get sacked for this!

"And did you find Grandad Fred, Mr. Ramsbottom?" asked Miss Bagshot.

"Yes Miss Bagshot," replied Noah.

"Then I think it's time you ran off home. Your mum will be expecting you for tea. It is, after all, nearly half past three."

"Half past three? Oh no, I'm late! Sorry, got to go. Thanks Littleplod, thanks Miss Bagshot— see you tomorrow!"

Noah turned and dashed out of the cave and into the bright winter sun. He could hear Littleplod pleading with Miss Bagshot as he clambered carefully over the ledge and down the crag. "I will be reporting you to Mr. Crockos for this, Littleplod!"

"Oh no, Miss Bagshot, not Mr. Crockos. Anyone but Mr. Crockos."

"Away with you!" Miss Bagshot waved the still-protesting Cave Guard away.

Noah ran as fast as he could all the way home.

"Mum, Mum, you'll never believe it!" he yelled as he flew into the farmhouse kitchen.

"Three-forty-five. I would Noah Ramsbottom, I would. You would say anything, but I told you to be back by three. So wash your hands, sit down, and have your tea."

"Oh Mum, but—"

"But nothing—not another word, my boy. You'll be in big trouble when your dad gets home!"

As Noah munched his sandwiches he could feel something in his pocket—it was Grandad's pipe!

"It was all real, I didn't dream it," he said quietly.

"What was that?" asked his mum.

"Nothing. Mum?"

"Yes."

"Can I go exploring on the hills tomorrow?"

"Only if you're back in time for tea!"

Lightning Source UK Ltd.
Milton Keynes UK
UKOW020714190712

196248UK00004B/21/P